Owl Girl

Mary Atkinson

Owl Girl

ISBN: 978-1-63381-059-4

cover artwork by
Jamie Hogan
www.jamiehogan.com

designed and produced by
Maine Authors Publishing
Rockland, Maine
www.maineauthorspublishing.com

Printed in the United States of America

For Amanda and, now, Julia

Owl Girl

Chapter One

Holly loved driving through Maine in summertime. She loved passing miles of leafy green trees. She loved the back roads curling into the hills like ribbons. She loved the endless sky. Whenever Holly came to the countryside, she felt light inside, like she could spread her arms and fly.

But not this time. This time she felt weighed down with worry.

She sat in the backseat with her dog, Bonk, and her older brother, Nick. Nick had ignored her the whole way, of course, listening to his iPod and reading his stupid car magazines.

Bonk laid his big black Lab head in her lap. Good ole Bonk. He always knew how to make her feel better. She took one of his ears and flipped it back and forth between her fingers. It was warm and velvety and calmed the jittery feeling in her stomach.

A little bit.

Soon the row of mailboxes with the little red flags whizzed past. Almost there, she thought.

Next came the sign pointing the way: Padgett Lake—Turn Right. Dad drove the car off the paved road and onto the dirt one. Barely a mile to go. Usually, this was where she'd sit up to look out the window, super excited about spending two lazy summer weeks at the lake with Gram and Gramp.

But not this year.

This year Mom and Dad weren't staying. This year they were going away on their own vacation. Holly slid Bonk's head off her lap and leaned forward. She tapped Mom on the shoulder in the front seat. "Do you and Dad have to?" she asked.

"Have to—?"

"Go to that lodge," Holly said.

"Yes, sweetie. Remember I told you? Sometimes moms and dads need time to themselves," Mom said.

Sure, she remembered what Mom had told her about going on vacation alone with Dad. But she also remembered overhearing Mom's conversations with Gram on the phone. About the "troubles" she and Dad were having. About the "rough patch" they were going through. About how they could use a little time together to work things out.

But sometimes, Holly knew, parents didn't work things out. Like her friend Liza's parents. Now Liza had to go back and forth between her mom's and dad's houses.

"You and Dad can have plenty of time to yourselves at Gram and Gramp's. Nick and I won't bother you. Right, Nick?"

Nick turned a page in his magazine.

She poked him in the side. "Right, Nick?" she shouted.

"Huh?" He slipped out one of his ear buds.

"You'll be fine, sweetheart," Mom said.

Holly crossed her arms over her chest. "No I won't. Nick won't play with me. And Gram never lets me do anything."

Worrywart Gram with her manners and rules. It was okay when Mom was around, but when Gram was in charge, she never let Holly do anything.

Mom turned around and looked at her. "I'm counting on you, Holly. To be a good sport," she said. "Can you do that for me?"

"I guess."

"Promise? Pinkie-swear?"

No way she wanted to be a good sport, but when she saw the asking look in Mom's eyes, she linked pinkies. "Promise," she said. "Pinkie-swear."

After Mom's finger slid away, Holly opened her car window and took in a deep breath of air. All along Padgett Lake Road, the trees and ferns and wildflowers danced in the breeze. A chipmunk darted into the woods. Clumps of fat blackberries dangled from bushes, waiting to be picked.

Suddenly, she itched to get out of the car. "Can I start walking now?" she asked.

"Do you remember the way?" asked Mom.

Dad stopped the car. "Of course she remembers the way. We've been coming up here ever since she was born."

"I meant," Mom said in the impatient voice she used with Dad these days, "that all these camp roads look the same. She might make a wrong turn. She could get lost."

"Don't be ridiculous. You're not going to get lost, are you, Holly?" Dad's eyes met hers in the rear-view mirror.

Were they going to get into a fight now, even about this, even about her?

Nick coiled his ear buds around his iPod and

put them in his pocket. "I'll take Holly," he said.

"Thank you, Nick," said Mom.

"I don't need anyone to take me. I'm not a baby."

Nick opened his car door. "Come on, Holly. I'll race you."

Holly got out of the car and Bonk followed. His dog tags made jingle-jangly sounds as he jumped onto the road.

As the car disappeared down the road, and Nick adjusted the straps on his sandals, Holly tightened her fists. She forged ahead with Bonk lumbering by her side. But as soon as Nick caught up, Holly slowed down.

The scent of hot sun on pine needles filled the air. Pieces of Padgett Lake glittered through the trees like diamonds. A woodpecker *knock-knock-knocked* against a rotten tree.

"Hi, woodpecker. Hi, lake. Hi, trees," whispered Holly. Let Nick race ahead of her and get there first. He always won anyway, and this time, Holly was in no hurry.

Chapter Two

From the end of the driveway, Holly could see Dad and Gramp unloading the car. Bonk raced ahead of Holly, wagging his tail so hard it looked like he'd shake it off his body. Obviously, Bonk had no clue that Mom and Dad were about to leave.

Gramp kneeled down for a face-lick. "Where's your girl, Bonk? Left her at home, have you?" Gramp raised a hand to his eyes, pretending to look for Holly, but in all the wrong directions. "Holly! Holly, where are you?" he called.

"I'm right here, Gramp!" Holly said, laughing.

"Tom? Valerie?" Gramp turned to Mom and Dad. "You forgot Holly."

Dad scratched his head and looked around. "Shoot," he said. "How'd that happen?"

"Gramp! I'm over here! In the driveway!" Holly waved her hands in the air.

"Oh, goodness no, Frank. Do stop," said Gram. "You're scaring her. She's still at that age."

Still at what age? Holly thought. "I'm not scared, Gram. I know Gramp's just playing around."

"Then what was all that jumping up and down and carrying on about?" Gram asked.

"Having fun?" Holly peeked at Gram from around Gramp's shoulder as she received his warm hug. Oh, great. Worrywart Gram. Here we go.

"Be good, you two. Do whatever Gram and Gramp tell you," Mom said after the car was unpacked.

"Whatever?" Gramp said. He rubbed his chin. "Hm-m-m. I've got a pile of wood needs stacking, a stone wall I want built."

"Sure, Gramp. You bet. And I'll paint the house, too," Nick said.

Holly moved next to Mom and held her hand.

"Don't forget to help with the dishes," said Dad.

"And remember, we make our beds every day at Padgett Lake," Gram added. "Right when we get up."

Gram and her bed-making thing. Before breakfast. Before swimming. Practically before breathing. "Mom?" She pulled Mom away from the others.

Mom bent down and gave Holly a hug. She whispered in her ear, "You'll be fine."

Two weeks with Gram and not letting a speck of sand in the house. And putting games away the second you were done playing. And never, ever leaving a wet towel on the floor.

"Is everybody all right over here?" Gram joined their conversation.

"Everybody's fine, Ma. Holly's a little nervous is all."

"Nervous? Why, what's she got to be nervous about?" Gram said.

"Give us a moment." Mom put an arm around Holly and walked her down the driveway. "Look, Holly. I know Gram can be bossy." She rolled her eyes and chuckled. "I'm her daughter, remember? But she can be fun, too, don't you think?"

"I guess." Holly looked over to Gram. She was stroking Bonk's head and telling him what a good dog he was.

"Remember the fairy houses you and Gram made together last time?"

Holly nodded.

"And the applesauce cake with icing and sprinkles?"

Again, she nodded.

"And it's Padgett Lake. You love Padgett Lake," Mom said.

"I love Padgett Lake with you and Dad." Holly's lips began to quiver. Any second now she'd start crying. But when she saw Mom's eyes filling with tears, too, she bit her lip and stopped.

"I'm going to miss you, too, Holly. But there's no reason you can't have fun." Mom wiped the tears from her face with the back of her hand.

She'd never seen her mom cry before. And there was Nick, over by the picnic table, joking around with Gramp and Dad about cleaning out the basement, cutting down trees, washing windows. He had no idea that Mom was crying. She threw her arms around her. "It's okay, Mom. Don't worry about me. I'll have fun. I'll be good, too. I promise."

And she'd keep her promise. She'd be the best girl ever.

Chapter Three

"Who's ready for a swim?" Gramp asked.

"All riiiight!" said Nick.

"Padgett Lake, here we come!" Holly said.

Bonk woofed.

Gram lifted a suitcase. "After we unpack," she said.

"Can't we swim first?" Holly asked.

"Nope," said Gram, heading up the front steps.

"But…" Holly began.

Nick nudged her with his elbow and whispered, "Just do what she says. It'll only take a second."

Bonk followed everyone into the house and curled up on his mat in front of the fireplace. Holly trudged upstairs behind the others. *I'll be a good girl, I'll be a good girl,* she chanted in her head as she climbed the steps.

The room Holly stayed in had slanted ceilings and a skylight over the bed. The wallpaper looked as if someone had sprinkled it with a bouquet of tiny blue and yellow flowers. A picture of a canoe that Mom had painted when she was a little girl hung on the wall. A pile of old children's books waited on the bedside table.

Holly took a deep breath of the lake air coming through the screened windows and began to unpack. First, she spread her red and yellow calico quilt on the bed.

"You don't still carry around that old thing, do you?" Gram asked as she came into the room. "I'm amazed it's in one piece."

"Mom helped me sew the rips," Holly said, pointing out her zigzag stitches.

Gram raised her eyebrows. "I can see she did."

Holly stuffed pajamas, socks, and underwear in one drawer. She grabbed an armful of shorts and T-shirts and jammed them in another. Finally, she crammed the rest of her clothes in the third drawer.

"Done!" Socks and sleeves and pant legs hung limply from each drawer. A sweatshirt's hood peeked out from under the dresser. In the hall, Gramp and Nick were already in their swimsuits, towels slung over their shoulders. She glanced into Nick's room. His clothes were piled on top of a rumpled bed. He and Gramp were heading down the stairs.

"Oh, Holly, do take care when you unpack," Gram said.

"Mom says on vacation it doesn't matter," Holly said.

Gram scooped up an armful of clothes and placed them on the bed. "Here, I'll help you fold."

"Can't I go now, Gram, please?" Through the open window she could hear Nick calling for Bonk.

"We'll do it now. Then it'll be done."

Out the window, she could see Nick, Gramp, and Bonk heading down the path to the lake, while here she was, standing next to Gram, folding her clothes as fast as she could. It wasn't fair. Nick got to go with Gramp while she was stuck with Gram. She knew it wasn't nice to think like that, but she couldn't help it.

"Hurry up, Bonk," she heard Nick cry. "Get your stick and come on!"

Holly gritted her teeth and kept folding.

Chapter Four

Gramp, Nick, and Bonk were already in the water, swimming to the raft, when Holly and Gram arrived on the dock. Holly tossed her towel on a tree branch. "Did you see the loon, Gram?"

"Oh, yes. We have four this year! A new record. And Holly. Listen. Do you hear?" Gram asked.

Ra-a-a-a-a-a. Ra-a-a-a-a-a. Holly heard a harsh rattling sound. "What is that?" she asked.

"See that bird? There, on that branch?" Gram said, pointing. "It's called a kingfisher."

The bird looked so funny with his pointy beak and ragged crest. "He looks like he could use some hair gel!"

"Notice how small his feet are. Synadactyl feet, they call them," Gram said.

Holly didn't know about his feet, but she liked watching the blue and white kingfisher plunge into the water. Soon he came out with a small fish in his mouth and flew back to his branch. "Look, Gram, he got a fish!"

"Sy-na-dac-tyl," Gram continued. "That's two toes partly joined together."

Sy-na-whatever. Why did Gram always have to turn everything into a lesson? Holly sat on the dock's edge, staring down at her own toes, wiggling them in the clear water. Gram settled on an Adirondack chair and opened her book.

"Not too hot, not too cold, just right," Holly said. That's what Mom always said when she went swimming in Padgett Lake. She sure wished Mom were here to swim with her now. To hold hands and bump butts under water, giggling when they came to the surface only to start the game all over again.

She climbed backwards down the dock ladder and into the water. She spun around, swirling her arms through the cool water, dance-kicking her legs. Then she floated on her back and looked up.

The clouds were her mirror, floating in the sky. She was just one small girl in a big beautiful world of water, earth, sky, trees, birds....

Gram's voice interrupted her thoughts. "Stay with me, Holly. Wait for Gramp," she said.

"Don't worry, Gram. I know how to swim really well now. Mom took me for lessons at the Y," she said.

"Swimming in a pool and swimming in the lake are two different things," Gram said. "Frank!" she called to Gramp. "Come get Holly."

Holly plunked herself down on the dock. Why did Gram have to be so bossy all the time? Fold your clothes. Take the beach towel, not the bath towel. Don't go barefoot. Stay on the dock.

A dragonfly flew in and settled on her knee. "Hi, dragonfly," she said. His clear, lacy wings didn't move. Holly looked into the dragonfly's bulging round eyes. "Getting ready for takeoff? Me, too!"

Soon Gramp swam back for Holly. "Come on, Hol'," he said. "Let's see you swim."

Holly pushed off and reached her arms through the silky water. She turned her head to breathe. Reach, roll, breathe. Reach, roll, breathe. Just like they'd taught her. She kicked harder and faster. Reach, roll, breathe.

Then she got a mouthful of water.

She stopped and coughed and sputtered and looked around for Gramp. She couldn't see him anywhere. The dock was way off to the side, not where it should be.

"Gramp?" she cried. She kicked her legs, treading water. "Gramp? Gramp?" She couldn't catch her breath. Her feet couldn't find the sandy bottom of the lake.

In a second, Gramp was by her side. "Climb on," he said. She wrapped her arms around his neck and got on his back. Just like when she was a little kid. "You swam a little crooked is all," he said.

Suddenly, the raft—with Bonk swimming around it and Nick jumping off of it—seemed very far away.

Gram waved a hand in the air. "Yoo-hoo! Frank! Are you sure she's ready? It's way over her head."

"You game?" Gramp asked Holly.

The Y pool was way over her head, too. Holly looked back at Gram and scrunched her lips. "Game," she said.

"That's my girl," Gramp said. He swam her to the raft. He set her on the ladder and she climbed up. A dripping wet Bonk climbed up after her. While Gramp and Nick kept jumping and diving in the water, Holly sat with Bonk at the very center of the rocking raft. She still had that nervous, jumpy feeling from not being able to catch her breath. She still felt the sting of water up her nose.

Nick stood on the raft's very edge. He hung on by his toes and waved his arms in the air. "Bet you can't push me in," he said to Holly.

"Can too," Holly said.

"Yeah? Let's see." He jumped around on the raft, rocking it, taunting her. He was playing around with her like he used to—and still did sometimes when none of his friends were around and it was just the two of them.

She popped up and gave Nick a good, strong push. "Aieeee!" Nick yelled. Bonk started barking. Holly giggled as he made a big show of losing his balance, arms flailing and legs thrashing, before finally falling into the water. Bonk jumped next. Holly threw a glance at Gram on shore, then held her nose, and jumped in, too.

Chapter Five

As Holly dried herself off outside—no dripping in the house, of course—she heard Gram talking to Bonk. "Getting some gray hairs, are you, ole Bonky boy? That's okay. Happens to all of us."

Holly heard the thump of Bonk's tail.

Gram continued. "What a good dog you are. Are you hungry? Is that it? Want some sup-sup? Grammy will get you some."

Grammy? Sup-sup? Holly wiped out her ears to make sure she'd heard right. Maybe if she had a tail to wag and could sit at attention, Gram would use that sweet voice on her, too.

Gram's pasta sauce bubbled on the stove, filling the kitchen with sweet tomato-ey smells. Holly's stomach began grumble. One thing about Gram, she sure knew how to cook. And one thing about Holly, after all that swimming, she sure was hungry.

"You set the table, and Nick will clear," Gram said to Holly.

Holly hummed as she arranged the mats on the table. She set out four plates. She folded the napkins in different shapes—a rectangle for Gramp, a square for Gram, and triangles for her and Nick. She placed knives, forks, and spoons in a different order around each plate.

Gram brought a breadbasket filled with warm bread. She looked at the table. "Oh, no, no, no, Holly," Gram said, laughing. "Don't you know? The forks go on the left." She fixed one setting. "And the knife and spoon go on the right."

"'Course I know how to set the table, Gram, but it's Sunday supper," Holly said. "On Sunday you can set the table any way you want. Sometimes we have no-utensil nights at our house, too."

"I'm sure you do. But, in our house on Sundays, we set the table the right way," Gram said. She gathered the rest of the utensils and handed them to Holly. "Finish up, now. We're just about ready to eat."

Did Gram really think Holly didn't know how to set a table? She was practically eight years old and Gram was still treating her like a baby. But Holly put the knives, forks, and spoons where they belonged. She'd promised Mom she'd be good and she would keep her promise.

• • •

That night, after Holly had washed her face, brushed her teeth, and got into bed, Gram began reading the first chapter from an old children's book called *The Wind in the Willows*. She made all the animal voices—Mole, Water Rat, Otter, and Badger. Holly felt like she was at the riverbank with Mole and his friends. She was rolling in warm grass, rowing Water Rat's boat, listening to river stories.

Gram finished the chapter and closed the book.

"Another chapter? Please?"

"Tomorrow." Gram smoothed Holly's covers.

"But Gram, I'm not tired."

"With all the swimming and running around you've done today, you'll be asleep in no time," Gram said.

"Nick's still up," Holly said.

"Nick's older. Door open or closed?"

Nick was twelve. Nick was always older. "Open," Holly said, sighing.

Gram gave her a kiss, and then turned off the light and left the room.

• • •

It was still light outside. A handful of stars blinked in the sky and the moon was three-quarters full. A rich, musty smell from the lake drifted through the window screens. Waves lapped along the shore.

Holly tossed and turned. She squeezed her eyes shut and counted up to ten and back down again to zero.

She could hear Nick playing chess with Gramp downstairs. Gram said Holly was too young. She said Holly needed to learn to sit still long enough before anyone could teach her a game like chess. Tap-tap-tap went the chess pieces. "Queen takes rook, checkmate!" Nick's voice traveled up the stairs.

A breeze lifted the curtains from the window. Holly got her quilt from the foot of the bed and hugged it in her arms. She buried her face in it and breathed in. It smelled like Mom's hand lotion and towels when they first came out of the dryer. Her quilt smelled like home.

If only Mom were here to rub her back and sing to her, then maybe she could sleep. A lump rose in Holly's throat. She swallowed hard and changed position. She squeezed her quilt tighter. A few tears spilled on her pillow.

Just then, from deep in the woods, came a distant call. Holly sat up. *Hoo-hoo, hoo-hoo; hoo-hoo, hoo-hoo-aww*. An owl. *Hoo-hoo, hoo-hoo; hoo-hoo, hoo-hoo-aww*. It was a mysterious sound, a hollow sound. It was as if the owl was calling from his tree, through the starry night, and into her room. Calling directly to her. Sending a message.

Downstairs, Bonk started barking.

"It's all right, Bonk, my boy," Gram said. "That's just a noisy old owl."

Hoo-hoo, hoo-hoo; hoo-hoo, hoo-hoo-aww, the owl sang. Holly got up and stood by her window. Her eyes searched the trees, silhouettes now against the darkening sky.

Hoo-hoo, hoo-hoo; hoo-hoo, hoo-hoo-aww.

The owl was lonely, too.

"Don't worry, Mr. Owl," Holly whispered. "I'm here."

She opened the drawer to the bedside table. She got out the flashlight Gram said was for emergencies if the power went out. She put on her flip-flops. She clicked on the flashlight and headed downstairs. White circles danced on the ceiling and walls. In the hall she turned off the flashlight and moved toward the porch.

"Holly? Is that you?" Gram asked.

Holly froze.

"Holly?" Gram repeated. "Is everything all right?"

She took small quiet footsteps to the porch. Bonk ran over and stood by her side. "Sure, Gram," she said sweetly. "Everything's fine."

"You weren't thinking of going outside, were you? Not at this hour," Gram said.

"There's an owl. Just outside my window. I wanted to see if I could find him. I think he's lonely," Holly said.

"Oh, give me a break," Nick said without looking up from the chess game.

Gram left her book on the chair and got up. She put her hands on Holly's shoulders, turned her around, and steered her back to the stairs. "Owls don't get lonely," she said.

"This one is."

"I'm sure he has plenty of friends out there," Gramp said.

Nick chuckled.

How dare he laugh at her?

"And owls are practically impossible to sight," Gram continued. "Holly, your owl friend will be just fine. Now, back to bed with you. Shall I take you?"

"No, Gram. I'm fine." Holly flapped her flip-flops back up the stairs and into her room. The flashlight rolled around in the drawer after she closed it. She got back into bed. She lay very still and listened and waited.

Before long, the owl called again: *hoo-hoo, hoo-hoo; hoo-hoo, hoo-hoo-aww. Hoo-hoo, hoo-hoo; hoo-hoo, hoo-hoo-aww.*

Gram was wrong. That owl was too lonely. He was calling out to Holly and she was going to find him.

Chapter Six

The next morning, Holly sat outside on the front steps with Bonk, finishing up her third piece of Gram's homemade cinnamon toast. Bonk stared at the toast and he stared at Holly. They weren't allowed to feed Bonk from the table, but this was outside. This was vacation. She pulled off a crust and accidentally let it slide through her fingers. Bonk dove for it. It didn't even reach the ground.

"I saw that." Nick pushed the screen door open and joined Holly on the stoop.

"So?"

"So, don't get all defensive. I'm not going to tell." Nick rolled his eyes in Gram's direction, where she stood inside at the sink doing the dishes. Then he tossed his unfinished toast in Bonk's direction. Bonk snapped it up and looked to Nick for more. "Sorry, buddy, that's it," Nick said.

"Want to go exploring?" Holly asked. "Remember last year we found those old glass bottles that Gramp said were like fifty years old?"

"They were only root beer bottles," Nick said. Only root beer bottles! He hadn't thought that way last year. Not when they were cleaning out the gunk inside with a hose. Not when they were finally able to read the label. Not when they added them to Gram's collection of Padgett Lake bottles. "Besides, Gramp needs me to help him with something."

Just then, Bonk started barking and running down the driveway. Holly heard the rumble of a truck coming down the road. Soon an open bed truck from Hoskins Hardware turned into their driveway. It was loaded with stacks of lumber. Gramp came outside and waved to the driver. "Morning, Bill. Don't worry about the dog," he called above the engine's rattle.

"Not with his tail going like that," Bill said out his open window. He turned off the engine and got out of the truck. As Gramp signed the yellow delivery slip, Bill glanced over at Holly and Nick. "Got yourself a pair of workers, I see," he said.

Gramp handed back the clipboard. "Two fine workers," he said.

"What're you going to build?"

"Peg's been asking me for a proper wood chest for the house," said Gramp.

"That'll come out real nice in this white pine," said Bill. "Easy to work with, too," he added, nodding his head toward Holly and Nick.

"You got that right," said Gramp.

Bill got back in the truck. "Have a good one," he said, waving out the window as he drove away.

"Come on, you two. Let's get cracking," Gramp said. "We need to saw these pieces in half." He handed Holly the measuring tape.

Holly held one end and Nick held the other.

"Eight feet," Nick said.

"So, half would be four," Holly said.

"D'uh." Nick gave Holly a look.

She shot his look right back.

Gramp made a mark on the wood with his flat carpenter's pencil. Then he drew a straight line with a ruler. One by one, Holly and Nick carried each board over to the picnic table. Gramp directed them to balance each piece on the bench and to sit on it. He grabbed a saw and cut the overhanging piece neatly along his pencil line.

"Can I try?" Nick asked.

"I thought you'd never ask," said Gramp.

Holly sat on the next piece of wood as Gramp taught Nick to saw. "Hold tight. Keep your eye on the pencil line. Keep your other hand out of the way. Bear down but give it a light touch. Keep the saw gliding back and forth. That's it, sure and steady," he said, guiding Nick's arm as he sawed.

"That's a good strong arm you've got there," Gramp said when Nick was done. "Try it by yourself." Nick sawed the next piece.

And the next piece. And the next piece. While Holly sat on the wood. She started kicking her dangling feet.

"Stay still, will you, Holly?" Nick asked.

"Gramp, can I have a turn?" Holly asked.

"Sure," said Gramp. "Let's see what kind of muscle you've got in your arm."

Gramp held the saw with Holly. She watched as their nice even strokes cut through the wood and added powdery sawdust to the pile on the ground. She listened to the shh-shh sounds of the saw. Sawing with Gramp was fun.

Gram opened the door and stood on the front stoop. "Frank, I really don't think Holly should be handling the saw," she said, approaching the picnic table.

"Look, Gram. I cut two pieces," Holly said. "You sit this time, Gramp. I'll do the next one by myself."

"Holly," Gram said. "Come help me with my loaves of bread."

"I don't want to make bread. I want to saw wood. Can I, Gramp?" she asked.

"It's all right, Peg. I'll stand right by her."

Holly lined up the saw right next to the pencil line and pushed down. The saw jumped out of place. She took a breath and tried again. Same thing. Stay still, she thought.

"Frank," Gram said.

"Here, let me get it started for you," Gramp said. He made a notch in the wood and handed Holly the saw. But as much as she tried, Holly couldn't get it going with those nice smooth strokes like she had with Gramp.

"I'll do it," Nick said.

"The dough's all ready to punch down, Holly," Gram said. "That's your favorite part."

"Give me the saw," Nick said.

"No," Holly said. "*I'll* do it." She looked at Gramp and added, "With Gramp." From then on, whenever it was her turn, Gramp helped her cut through the wood. There was no way Holly was going to let Nick have all the turns. And there was no way she was going to give in to Gram.

Chapter Seven

After lunch it was time to put the chest together. Once again, Gramp started out hammering the nails, Nick asked for a turn, Gramp helped him, and soon Nick was happily hammering away on his own. And once again, Holly asked if she could try, Gramp helped her, and then she tried on her own. But when the nails went in crooked and two times she almost smashed her thumb, she handed the hammer back to Gramp.

"Come on, Bonk. Let's go exploring," she said.

Bonk slowly lifted himself from his place in the sun, stretched, and followed her down the driveway. When they got to the dirt road, Holly paused. "Right or left?" she asked. Bonk sniffed the air, looked at Holly, and turned left.

Soon they came to an overgrown camp road. It was deeply rutted with clumps of long grass growing down the middle. "Let's go here," she said.

They walked on until the sound of Nick's hammer pounding the nails faded in the distance. They came to a small clearing with a pile of rotting firewood and an overturned rusty metal chair. Holly yanked the chair out of the dirt, brushed it off, and sat down.

This would be her secret place. Her place where she could do whatever she wanted. With no one—not Gram or Nick—to bother her. Next time, she'd bring some snacks, dog biscuits for Bonk, a water bottle, and some books to read.

While Bonk found a new patch of sun to lie in, Holly cleared old sticks and tossed them aside. She gathered rocks and shaped them into a sculpture. She stuffed her pockets with tiny pinecones. She hummed the songs she learned in Kids' Chorus at school.

She was sitting on the chair, feeling the sun on her shoulders and a gentle wind through her hair, when she sensed something deep in the woods. She didn't see it or hear it. She felt it in the air—something moving, like a whispery cloud. Or a ghost.

She turned her head left and right, looked high and low, and saw only a flicker of leaves. She slowly turned her head again. Large shadowy wings were rising and falling, rising and falling, then disappearing up, over, and beyond the trees.

Her owl? Come to find her? It had to be. Holly stepped lightly through the woods. She looked high and low, through the trees and up to the sky. "Hey, Mr. Owl," Holly called. "Come back. I'm right here!" She walked deeper into the woods, keeping her ears open, straining her eyes to see.

Bonk wandered behind her. "Shhhh, Bonky," she whispered. "That's my owl. We have to be really quiet." She held her breath as she watched its waving wings disappear behind the trees.

Hooonk!! A car horn blasted the silence. Bonk started barking. Darn! Now the owl would fly away for sure.

Then came Gram's voice. "Holly? Holly! Where are you?" she yelled through the trees.

Holly got back on the path and started running. "What's wrong, Gram?" she asked when she got to the car.

"What's wrong? You can't run off like that, Holly. I didn't know where you were," said Gram.

"Don't worry, Gram. I knew where I was the whole time. And guess what? I saw my owl."

"Nonsense. Owls don't fly around in broad

daylight," Gram said. "And what's this you've got all over your backside?"

Holly twisted to look over her shoulder. A mess of dirt and pine needles covered her shorts. She tried to brush it away but the pine needles were stuck on with sap.

"Oh Holly, what am I going to do with you?" Gram asked.

"Do with me?"

"Come. Now. Into the car. We're going back to the house to have a little talk."

"Yes, Gram," Holly said, as she picked pine needles off her shorts. She and Bonk followed Gram to the car. She swallowed hard at the thought of having a 'little talk' with Gram. But the flowing, fleeting image in the woods stuck in her mind. Daylight or not, she knew it was her owl.

When Holly and Gram got back to the house, Nick and Gramp were standing in the yard, drinking soda from cans, admiring their wood chest. "Hey, Holly," Nick called. "Come take a look!"

Bonk slid out of the car and ran over to Nick. Holly started to follow until she felt a hand on her shoulder. "Not now, Nick," Gram said. "Holly and I need to have some private time to talk about where she got off to."

"Sure, Gram. I understand," Nick said. Like he was a grownup instead of a kid. Holly felt herself shrink down to the size of a toad.

Gram sat Holly down with a plate of ginger cookies and a glass of lemonade. Bonk went to his place on the braided rug. "You seem to forget that you're only seven years old. And that it's my job to keep track of you," Gram said.

"I'm practically eight, Gram. You don't need to keep track of me all the time."

"I'm afraid I do." Gram sighed.

"I know my way around here. I won't get lost."

"Part of growing up is learning to think before you act. Like not sneaking out at night to look for owls. Or traipsing off without telling anyone. You might get hurt and we wouldn't know where to find you."

Holly felt her cheeks burn.

"From now on," Gram continued, "I want you to tell me or Gramp before you go wandering off on your own. I don't want you going any farther than the end of the driveway by yourself. And never out of earshot."

"What about down to the lake, Gram?" Holly asked. Her world was becoming smaller and smaller.

"If you go to the lake, I want you stay on the dock and out of the water," Gram said.

"Really, Gram. You don't have to worry so much," she said. "I know what I'm doing."

"I'm sure you think you do, but you're still a child and I'm in charge of you. Sometimes children start daydreaming and get carried away by their imaginations," said Gram.

"Yes, Gram. Can I, *may* I go now?" Holly asked.

"Now that we understand each other, right?" Gram's eyes seemed to look through hers right into the middle of her brain.

Holly nodded. "Bonk!" she called. From his place on the rug, Bonk raised his ears and flashed open his eyes. Within seconds he was by her side. At least there was someone who trusted her, even if he was a dog. She turned the doorknob.

"Holly?" Gram asked. "Are you forgetting something?"

No, she wasn't forgetting. Gram hadn't even given her a chance. "Bonk and I are going to the lake. But we won't go in the water, I promise."

Holly sat on the dock with Bonk and tossed the little pinecones she'd collected into the water. Being seven years old stunk. Turning eight would be good.

Nine even better. And ten? Ten would be perfect. She was sure of it. When she was ten, maybe then, Gram would let her be.

If only Mom were here and the boss of her, not Gram.

Ra-a-a-a-a. Ra-a-a-a-a. The kingfisher. She looked across the lake, trying to find the sound, but all she saw was water and trees.

Holly put an arm around Bonk and together they looked out. Missing Mom made her chest ache. And Dad, too. She wished they were here. Two loons swam by. She sure hoped Mom and Dad were working things out.

Chapter Eight

A few days later, Gramp was making a pile of peanut butter and jelly sandwiches in the kitchen for Nick's and his fishing trip while Holly sculpted clay at the table.

"You can do better than that, can't you Frank? There's turkey, tuna. I could make you chicken salad," Gram said.

"We'll be fine with these, right Nick?" Gramp said.

Nick looked up. "PB and J? No problem," he said.

Holly rolled her clay into a ball.

Gramp stuffed all the sandwiches in a plastic bag and put them in the cooler.

"How about some carrots?" Gram held up a bag of baby carrots.

"Carrots? Fishermen don't eat vegetables,"

Gramp said. But he kissed Gram on the cheek and added the carrots to the cooler anyway.

"Hey, Gramp. Can we stop at that little store in town like last year?" Nick asked.

"You bet. Only place for jerky, coke, and pork rinds," Gramp said. Gram let out a groan.

Holly pinched the clay to make an owl's beak. "I don't see why I can't go," she said.

"You wouldn't last for two seconds in a boat," said Nick. "Try a whole day. You'd be whining to come home as soon as you got there."

"No, I wouldn't," said Holly.

"See? Precisely my point."

"Don't worry, Hol'," Gramp said, ruffling her hair. "You and I will have our own private fishing trip later. Probably catch more fish, too."

"Besides," Gram said to Holly. "I need your help picking blueberries and making pies."

"Blueberry pie? All riiiight," said Nick.

Holly pressed the tip of her baby finger into the clay two times to make two owl eyes. She liked blueberry pie, too. But berry picking with Gram? Fishing with Gramp and Nick sounded like a lot more fun.

• • •

At the end of the camp road, the two cars split off in different directions, Gramp and Nick to Grand Lake, and Holly and Gram to Midge's U-Pick 'Em. Bonk stayed at home, happily chewing on the dog-chewy Holly insisted on giving him after Gram said dogs weren't allowed at Midge's.

As Gram drove, piano music poured from the car radio in rolling waves like the winding country roads. Holly looked out her open window at the cloudless, postcard-blue sky. Warm summer air rushed by her face and blew through her hair.

Soon Gram turned off the paved road onto a dirt road up a steep hill. At the top of the hill was a sign: "Midge's U-Pick 'Em, Next Left." Holly sat up. Gram parked by a small white house with green shutters. A blue plastic tarp hung over a picnic table, leaving it in the shade. At the table sat a woman Gram's age surrounded by boxes and crates. She was drinking iced tea.

The woman had a nice smile and sparkly eyes. Holly read the sign behind her. It read: Welcome to Midge's U-Pick 'Em! Pick all you can. Take as many boxes as you want. $3 per quart. Please watch your kids. Please, no pets.

"Where are the berries?" Holly asked, looking around and seeing none.

"Follow the arrows," Midge said, "around back of the barn."

A series of faded blueberry-blue arrows painted on old barn wood signaled the way.

"Wow!" Holly said when she saw row upon row of bushes as tall as she was in a seemingly endless field. She had seen blueberries before but none like these. Some looked as big as marbles. A sweet, fruity scent filled the air. Holly was itching to dive in.

"These are called high bush blueberries, Holly. They're different from the wild…" Gram began to explain.

But Holly had stopped listening. She took off, running and skipping down the rows, breathing in the air, listening to the birds, feeling the warm sun on her arms. At the end of a row, she took a left, then a right. Out of breath, she stopped. She grabbed a fistful of berries and crammed them into her mouth. Then another. And another. They were warm and sweet and tart all at the same time.

"Holly!" Gram called. "Where are you? Come back here!"

Holly dropped her handful of berries. She raced back.

"Don't disappear on me like that, Holly. We've got berries to pick."

"I'm sorry, Gram."

"And what's that all over your face and shirt? Oh, I might have known," Gram said.

Holly looked down at her T-shirt. Covered in blue.

"Somebody's got to fill these boxes if we want pie, you know," Gram said.

Holly noticed sweat trickling down Gram's face. She was rubbing the back of her neck as if it was hurting her.

Holly remembered what Mom had said about wearing Gram out. "Have you tasted the berries? You're allowed to take a break, you know," she said. She picked a fresh handful and held them out to Gram. "Try them. Right now. And give me that box. I'll fill it."

Gram handed the box to Holly and ate a handful of berries. "Mmmmm," she said, smiling. "Those are good. Warm and sweet as a day in August."

Holly scooped another handful of berries from the box. "Have some more," she said.

"Not from the box," Gram cried.

"Relax, Gram. With me helping and all these

berries," Holly said, sweeping an arm through the air, "we can fill a hundred boxes in no time."

Gram lowered herself to sit on the ground and Holly got to work. No need for Mom worrying about any of her energy wearing Gram out.

Chapter Nine

That night after dinner, Holly sat outside with Nick on the front steps, her belly close to bursting from a fish fry supper and two pieces of blueberry pie. Inside, Gram and Gramp listened to the radio. Waves of their quiet conversation drifted out the screened windows onto the stoop.

"What do you think Mom and Dad are doing right now?" Holly asked.

"How should I know?" Nick picked up a stick and broke it in little pieces.

"They're probably eating dinner, don't you think?" Holly asked.

"Hm-m-m."

"Talking about the favorite part of their day."

"Yeah, probably."

"You know, the way we do at home."

Nick got up and walked over to the hammock. He

lay down and wrapped the hammock around him like a cocoon, sticking out one hand to pull on the rope until the hammock swung back and forth high in the air.

Holly watched as the sun slipped behind the hills and the sky began to deepen from light blue to purplish blue. Bats swooped and dipped and tittered about, looking for insects.

A motorboat puttered past on the lake. Holly pulled up a long piece of grass and began tying it in knots. Then she grabbed handfuls of grass and threw them into the air. "Hey, Nick! I have an idea. Let's go looking for my owl!"

"Your owl?" Nick asked.

"From the other night? Want to go find him?"

"Holly. Just because you hear the owl and he sounds close by, doesn't mean he is. He could be in the hills, across the lake, in the next town over for crying out loud."

"He's right down the road."

Nick stopped the hammock and sat up. "How do you know?"

"Because I know," she said. "Please, Nick? Gram'll never let me go by myself."

"Oh, all right," Nick said. He headed to the house. "I'll tell Gram."

"And get two flashlights," Holly said.

While Nick was inside, Holly stood listening. Night sounds filled her ears: the deep rumbling of bull-frogs, the low voices of fishermen on the lake, loons calling in the distance. "Hey, Mr. Owl, where are you?" she whispered. She turned her head to listen.

Hoo-hoo, hoo-hoo; hoo-hoo, hoo-hoo-aww.

She knew it. Her owl was waiting right down the road. She could barely keep her feet still. What was taking Nick so long?

Nick returned with two headlamps from Gramp and a watch from Gram to make sure they'd be back in a half-hour.

They didn't really need the headlamps. It was still light enough to see, and what light nighttime was taking from the sky, the rising moon was quickly putting back.

"We're on our way, Mr. Owl," Holly called out.

"Will you be quiet?" Nick said in a fierce whisper. "How do you expect to find an owl if you're making all that noise?"

Holly had to admit that Nick was right on this one. They continued walking in silence. Fireflies blinked and disappeared. The air turned cooler.

Hoo-hoo, hoo-hoo; hoo-hoo, hoo-hoo-aww.

Holly pointed into the woods. "It's coming from right over there."

"You're crazy, know that?" Nick said.

They stepped off the dirt road onto a woodland floor of pine needles and fallen leaves. Without the openness of the road and with the tall trees stretching high and blocking the moonlight, the night grew darker.

Holly stumbled over the limb of a rotten tree. Nick stepped on a branch, breaking it in half, craaaack!

"Shhhh!" Holly said.

"This is ridiculous. We're never going to see an owl. We'd better turn back," said Nick.

Hoo-hoo, hoo-hoo; hoo-hoo, hoo-hoo-aww, the call got louder.

"Turn back? But we're almost there," said Holly.

"We've been gone twenty minutes," said Nick.

"So?" Holly strained her ears in the silence.

"Gram'll have a fit if we come in late," said Nick.

Holly groaned. "I guess you're right. We'd better go."

But as they turned to leave, Holly sensed something. Just like before, she didn't see it or hear it: she felt it deep inside. She looked up to see large shadowy wings, lifting above the treetops, into the night.

She grabbed Nick's arm. "Look, Nick. My owl." She pointed into the sky.

Nick looked up. "Wow, Holly, you're right."

"See? I told you we'd find him. I knew all along he was close by. And I was right. I told you!"

• • •

"Gram! Gramp!" Holly pushed her way through the front door. "We saw him! Nick saw him, too!" she yelled. Gramp looked up from tying fishing flies. Gram rested her book in her lap.

"Who did you see?" Gramp asked.

"My owl. Lost and lonesome, far from home." Holly sighed.

Nick glared at her. "Lost and lonesome? Give me a break. You are so weird."

Holly clamped her mouth shut. *Children start daydreaming. They get carried away by their imaginations.* Gram's words came back to her.

"Owls are not like those cartoon characters you

kids watch on television. They're wild animals. They can be very dangerous," Gram said. She pulled one of her bird books from the bookcase. "Come sit by me, Holly. Let's see what we can learn about owls."

Oh, great, lesson time, Holly thought, as she sat next to Gram on the couch. Gram flipped through the pages until she came to a picture of a brown owl streaked with white stripes. She showed Holly the page. "Is this the one you saw?"

"Yup," said Holly. "He looked just like that. 'Barred owl,'" she read. She stared at the picture. It had soft brown eyes and a pointy yellow beak. "'Some people think this owl's call sounds like the words, Who cooks for you? Who cooks for you all?'"

She started laughing. "Who cooks for you? Who cooks for you all?" she repeated. "This bird book is right. That owl sure did sound like he was talking about cooking." She looked at the next page. It had a picture of owlets in a nest. Maybe Mr. Owl wasn't alone. Maybe he had a family!

She lifted the book off her lap to show Gramp. "Look at him, Gramp. And see the baby owlets in the nest? Aren't they so cute?"

Gramp looked up from his flies. "Very cute."

"Owls are very protective of their young. Cute

as they are, they can get truly nasty," said Gram. "If you ever come across a nest, stay away. Isn't that right, Frank?"

"Absolutely."

Holly stared into the owl's all-knowing eyes. "Don't worry," she said. "If I ever find a nest, I'll definitely stay away."

Chapter Ten

The clock on Holly's bedside table said 5:45 when Gram woke her the next morning. She let out a big yawn. "Time to get up already?"

Gram nodded. "Remember? Today is bird watching day," she said. "I'm going to teach you the proper way to look for birds."

Holly rubbed the sleep from her eyes and slid out of bed. "Can we make blueberry pancakes for breakfast, Gram?" she asked.

"Certainly. But bird watching first, then breakfast. The birds are busiest in the early morning. Now wash up and get dressed. I'll meet you downstairs in five minutes."

Holly drank a glass of orange juice and ate a piece of toast: a birdwatcher's snack, Gram said, that would "hold her by."

Gram gathered water bottles, her bird book,

and a sketchbook. "This is for you," she said, handing Holly a black, hard-covered notebook. It was a real journal. Not a kid's journal. Holly stroked the cover. "It's for keeping track of all the birds you see.

"Next, binoculars." Gram's binoculars were hanging on their special peg in the mudroom along with rain jackets, badminton rackets, sun-hats, shopping bags, a net for catching minnows. "Binoculars are the most important piece of a birdwatcher's equipment," Gram said.

"Can I try them?" Holly reached out her hand.

"Yes, you *may,* after I show you how. And you're not to use them without me. Binoculars are an expensive instrument, not a toy, Holly." Gram removed the plastic caps and demonstrated how to adjust the eyepiece and turn the center wheel to focus.

"Never, ever touch the glass," Gram continued. "We don't want to scratch the lenses." She looped the strap around Holly's neck. "Always keep the strap around your neck. That way they won't fall."

Together, they set off down the road. Soon they arrived at Gram's favorite bird watching spot at the edge of the woods by a burbling brook and an open field. "Stand very still and observe," Gram said. It was a calm, sunny morning without a hint of a breeze. Birds were singing everywhere, it seemed, but Holly couldn't see even one.

"Over there," Gram whispered, pointing. "Watch how the branches bounce. There are two chickadees in that tree."

All Holly saw was a wall of green leaves. No birds.

"And who's that scurrying down the branch?" Gram whispered. Gram helped Holly locate the bird. "See how he goes down the tree head first? That's a nuthatch."

Holly zeroed in on the little blue-and-white bird. "He's upside-down with his tail up in the air. What a show-off." She giggled.

"He's looking for insects under the bark."

"Yum," Holly said.

Gram laughed.

Soon Gram was helping Holly identify more birds: woodpeckers, wrens, sparrows, and phoebes. Each time, she told Holly to write down their names in her notebook. Later, she could copy their pictures from the bird book. "You're starting your life list," she said.

"Life list?"

"Serious birders keep a list of all the birds they've seen."

While Gram kept looking for birds, Holly sat with her back against a tree. She opened her journal to a fresh page. 'Barred owl' she wrote in her neatest handwriting.

Chapter Eleven

A few days later, while Holly and Nick were playing gin rummy (Gram had asked Nick to play three games with Holly before he went out by himself on a canoe ride), Mom called.

"Oh, yes, Nick and Holly have settled in just fine," Gram said into the phone. "How are you and Tom doing? Finding time to get outside and enjoy this glorious weather?"

The room went quiet as Gram listened. At the table, Holly dealt out seven cards for each of them and then waited for Nick to make the first play. Mom sure was taking a long turn talking to Gram. "What's she saying?" she asked.

Gram held a finger to her lips.

Holly glanced at Nick. For a second, they shared a look.

"Oh, I see. Yes, that's hard. Well, I'm sure…"

Gram said.

Nick discarded a nine of hearts.

More silence as Gram listened. Then, "Hm-m-m, well, give it some time. You want to talk to the kids? They're right here."

Holly raced to the phone first. "Hi, sweetie, are you having fun?" Mom asked.

"Mom, I've seen three loons and Gram and I made applesauce cake."

"With the white icing and sprinkles on top?" Mom asked.

"Yup, and Gram said we can make ice cream, too, after we go into town to do some errands."

"Are you being good for Gram? Not wearing her out?"

"Don't worry. Everything's fine."

"Let me say hi to Nick."

"Okay. Bye, Mom. Here's Nick."

Nick told Mom about building the wood box with Gramp and how he'd passed Gramp's canoe test so he could go out in the canoe on his own. "Is Dad there? Can I talk to him?"

Holly had forgotten to ask to speak to Dad. And she'd forgotten to tell Mom about the owl. "Wait, I'm not done," she said. She reached for the phone.

Nick shook his head and pulled away. "Oh, okay."

"Where's Dad? I need to talk to Mom again."

Nick glared at her. No! he mouthed. "Oh. Okay. Yup. I will. Bye." He hung up the phone.

"Hey, I wanted to talk to her some more," Holly said.

"She had to go," Nick said.

"But what about Dad? What'd she say about Dad?"

"He wasn't there. Come on, let's finish our game."

"Not there? Where was he?"

"He had to go back to the city for work."

"For how long?"

"I don't know, Holly. Jeez, will you give me a break?"

"Just a couple of days," Gram said. "He's coming back soon."

They played their three games of rummy. Holly won two out of the three. It should've been fun, playing those games with Nick, and winning, but it wasn't.

So when Nick got up to go for his canoe ride, Holly begged to go with him. She promised to paddle just as much as he did, and she'd be very careful not to splash him with the paddle.

"Okay, fine," Nick agreed.

"Don't forget your life vests and stay in the cove, close to shore. No going beyond the Raymonds' dock. I want you back in one hour," Gram said, holding on to Bonk, who was not a good canoe passenger, as they went out the door.

The lake was calm as Holly and Nick set off in the canoe, Holly up front and Nick steering in the back. They stayed along the shore, just as Gram had told them, past the lily pads but in the shelter of the cove. They headed to Broken Tree Point, an outcropping of land they'd named years ago where the top of a tall pine tree had broken off in a storm.

Holly tried really hard to keep quiet and not chatter but sometimes when things got stuck in her mind, she couldn't help it. She twisted around on her seat and faced Nick. "Do you think Mom and Dad still love each other?"

"'Course they love each other. Parents fight sometimes. It's no big deal."

Holly told him all about how her friend Liza's father always went on trips for work and then he moved out and got his own house.

"You said you wouldn't jabber." Nick dug his paddle into the water, taking stronger and stronger strokes, jerking back and forth from both sides of the stern.

Holly twisted around to look at her brother. There were muscles on his neck and shoulders that didn't used to be there. He had a mean look on his face. The canoe jostled against the water, tipping from one side to the other, heading away from the shore. "What're you doing?" she yelled.

"Going for a canoe ride."

"Gram said not away from shore!"

"I don't care, dammit."

And he didn't used to swear. Holly faced front and dug her paddle into the water, too. She'd never seen Nick like this, so wound up that he might explode.

Away from the cove, Padgett Lake opened up into a body of water, so large that in some places Holly had to squint to make out the trees on the other side. Winds funneled in from the north, stirring up the water, making choppy waves and whitecaps. Holly's arms ached; she kept splashing herself with water.

"Turn around!" she yelled. She checked that her life vest was zipped to the top, the belt tight around her waist.

"No!"

“I want to go back,” Holly cried.

“Don’t be such a baby,” Nick said.

Cold water sprayed on Holly’s bare arm. Just then a gust of wind caught the bow. The canoe swerved off course. She fell off her seat.

“Get up and paddle hard,” Nick yelled.

“Take me home,” Holly screamed.

“Jeez, Hol’. There’s nothing to be scared of. Just paddle.”

She pulled hard on her paddle as Nick steered them to calmer waters.

“Take me to the Raymonds’ dock,” Holly cried. Her body shook all over.

Nick steered the canoe to their neighbors’ dock and let Holly off. “I’ll meet you back at the house. Don’t you dare tell Gram,” he said.

“Don’t worry.” She’d never tell Gram what had happened. Not in a million years. She walked along the edge of shore back to Gram and Gramp’s dock. She was already in trouble with Gram about wandering off on her own. If Gram found out about what Nick had done, she’d lock them both in the house and throw away the key.

Chapter Twelve

Rain was falling when Holly got out of bed the next morning. There was a chill in the house. She wrapped her red and yellow calico quilt around her shoulders. Today, she decided, would be a day for sketching birds in her journal, baking cookies, and playing Monopoly. Maybe she could get Nick to play if chocolate chip cookies were involved.

After yesterday, she really needed him to act normal again.

"Morning, Bonk," she called out when she reached the bottom step. Bonk thumped his tail on the floor, but didn't get up. "I said, 'Good morning, Bonk!'" Holly repeated, tapping her toe on the floor.

Bonk didn't move.

Holly went over to his doggy bed. "Bonk? What's the matter with you?" She crouched next to him. "Oh, Bonky, is a little rain making you lazy? Come on, boy. Get up!"

Bonk raised his head. He jiggled his tail. He dangled a paw off the edge of his cushion, but he didn't get up.

"Nick!" she called up the stairs.

Nick came down the stairs in his sweats, rubbing his eyes.

"There's something wrong with Bonk," she said.

Nick joined her at Bonk's cushion. "Come on, boy," Nick said. "Walk? Wanna go on a walk?"

Bonk looked at Nick, wagged his tail like he really didn't want to let anyone down, but still he didn't move.

Holly called for Gramp. Gramp petted Bonk's head, rubbed his shoulders and rump, and gently lifted him to stand. Bonk limped around the room, wagging his tail. Then he turned around and went back to bed.

"Poor Bonk," Gram said.

"I probably ran him too hard yesterday," Gramp said, "but all the same, we'd better take him into town. I'll call the vet."

They all piled into the car: Gram and Gramp up front, Bonk in between Holly and Nick in the back. Holly draped her calico quilt over Bonk's head and tucked it around his front paws.

"He's not a stuffed animal," Nick said.

"I'm just keeping him warm," Holly said.

"Like he needs to be kept warm." Nick put ear buds in to his ears and turned on his iPod.

What did Nick know? He didn't understand Bonk the way Holly did.

While Nick listened to his iPod, Holly stroked Bonk's ears and rubbed his neck. Whatever was wrong with him, she'd be there for him. She wouldn't let him down.

When they got to the animal clinic, Gramp put a leash on Bonk and gave him a little tug to get him moving out of the car. Holly followed Gramp and the slow-moving, limping Bonk into the building. In the clinic, she sat on the tile floor and reached under the chair to hold Bonk's paw.

"Take a seat, Holly," Gram said.

"But Bonk…"

"Children belong in chairs, not on the floor."

"Yes, Gram." Holly slid into a chair.

While they sat and waited, Nick paged through one of the animal magazines left on a table and Holly looked at the posters on the wall. There was one about dental care for dogs, another showing the skeleton of a horse, a third about wildlife rehabilitation with pictures of baby squirrels, raccoons, birds, rabbits, turtles.

Found an injured or orphaned animal?

LEAVE IT ALONE!

Call a Licensed Wildlife Rehabilitator.

Remember: ***All wild animals can be dangerous.***
Call **Padgett Animal Clinic** for more information.

Soon a tall woman with wavy black hair came out of the examining room. She wore a white coat and black pants. "Bonk Lawson?" she called.

Holly read her name, Dr. Susan Davis, D.V.M., embroidered on her jacket pocket with small animal paw prints all around it. "Bonk's right here," she said. "He's my dog and I noticed this morning that he's not feeling well."

"He's not just your dog," Nick said.

"Come with me and let's take a look," Dr. Davis said.

Gramp coaxed Bonk to get up, stroking his head and then gently pulling his leash to guide him into the examination room. Holly followed behind. Then she felt the familiar hand cupping her shoulder. Gram. "Gramp will go in with Bonk. You wait out here with us," she said.

She kicked her legs back and forth in her chair until Gram settled that same hand on her knee and asked her to please be still.

Holly fumed. If Mom or Dad were here, they'd let her go into the examination room. But they weren't here, were they? she thought. They were on their own vacation, trying to…she started kicking her legs again. She didn't want to think about Mom and Dad.

It seemed like forever before Gramp came out with Bonk. Holly ran up to them. "What happened? What's wrong with Bonk?" she asked.

"The doc's pretty sure it's Lyme disease, that Bonk got bit by an infected tick quite a while ago, and we're just seeing the effects of it now," Gramp said.

Dr. Davis brought two blue plastic bottles of medicine. "This one will help with the joint pain," she said as she handed the first one to Gramp, "and you can start him on these antibiotics as soon as the test proves positive. If he shies away from the pills, give them to him with a spoonful of peanut butter or a lump of cheese."

"Bonk's going to be okay, isn't he?" Holly reached down to rub his head, stroke his ears.

"Depends on how long he's been infected," Dr. Davis answered. "The medicine will get rid of the disease, but if he's had it for a while, it could've already damaged his joints. Plus, Bonk's not a young dog. Don't expect him to bounce back to be the way he used to be."

Bonk rested his head in Holly's lap on the way home. As she stroked his head, she thought about what Dr. Davis had said. That Bonk was getting old. His joints were creaky, it hurt him to run around and the Lyme disease had just made it worse. The pills she gave him would help with the pain, but he would never run around like a young dog again.

Holly couldn't wait to grow up. But she wanted Bonk to stop getting older. What if there was a way she could trade years with Bonk so she'd be older and he'd be younger? She thought about that some more. He'd lose the gray on his schnoz and belly. His joints wouldn't hurt. He'd have more energy. And she'd be, well, older, and older was better. No one would treat her like a little kid all the time. "Nick, listen to this. What if..." she began and presented her idea.

"What is your problem? Are you lame or what?" Nick said.

"I was only playing around." She shrunk back into her corner of the car.

"Why do you have to be so stupid all the time?" Nick said. His face reddened.

"Don't call me stupid! You're not supposed to say 'stupid'!" Holly yelled. "I'm going to tell Mom."

Gram shifted in her seat.

"Don't you get it?" Nick said. "Bonk's not going to live forever. He's old. He's going to die pretty soon."

"Shut up, Nick!" Holly screamed.

Gram turned around and glared at Holly. "Holly, calm down."

Holly's lips bunched together. She clenched her teeth.

"Nick's upset about Bonk. He probably doesn't want to joke around right now, do you Nick?" Gram said.

Nick shrugged his shoulders. He rubbed Bonk's head.

Rain washed down Holly's car window. If only she'd kept her mouth shut. Then Nick wouldn't be mad at her, Gram wouldn't have had to put her two cents in, and she wouldn't be thinking about Bonk getting old and dying.

Mom would've understood. Mom would've known she was just pretending, just trying out an idea.

And Mom would know what to say to take away the empty feeling that was now filling her chest.

Chapter Thirteen

By the time they got back to Padgett Lake, the rain had stopped, but a bank of heavy gray clouds hung in the sky. The clouds swirled and churned like they couldn't decide whether to open up to blue skies or start a new storm. While Holly was still fussing to unbuckle her seatbelt, Bonk followed Nick out of the car and into the house. Before Holly could even take her jacket off, Nick was settled in with Bonk, his head propped up on the cushion, reading a book.

Holly went upstairs to her room to be by herself—away from bossy Gram, away from know-it-all Nick. She sat at the small desk in her room and opened Gram's bird book to the barred owl. She began to copy its picture into her journal. She took her time to make each feather look just right.

Through her window, she could hear Gram and

Gramp talking on the screened-in porch down below.

"With all the commotion about Bonk, I never got to tell you about my call with Valerie this morning," Holly heard Gramp say.

"Oh?" said Gram.

"It was quite distressing."

Distressing? Holly perked up her ears.

"Valerie said they were talking about a separation."

"Oh, no," Gram groaned.

A separation? Liza's parents got a separation before they got a...The D word flitted around the room like an angry wasp.

"Things aren't going well," Gramp continued. "Valerie thinks she might need some time to herself."

Holly jumped up, toppling her chair against the desk. Pencils rolled off the table and clattered to the floor. She should pick them up. Do it now, then it'll be done, she imagined Gram saying. But she was going to burst if she didn't get outside. She didn't have time to pick up any darn pencils.

She snuck downstairs, past the porch and into the mudroom. There were Gram's binoculars hanging on their peg. Thoughts darted around in her head like stinging black flies. Distressing...separation...time to herself....

She eased the strap off the peg and around her neck. Her legs carried her, running out the door, down the driveway, to the place where she'd turned into the woods with Nick. She paused and looked back to the house.

No farther than the end of the driveway. No using the binoculars without her.

The heck with Gram and her stupid rules.

Holly stepped over the branch she'd stumbled on before and walked into the woods. The bird book said that the best place to look for owls was in old, rotting trees. Owls find nests that used to belong to hawks, crows, or squirrels. The owls move in and take them over as their own.

Every time Holly came to a rotting tree, she stopped and looked up. The woods were filled with old tree stumps and decaying trees, but no nests. She stretched her ears to listen for owls but heard only the fluttering of leaves and an occasional chickadee.

Discouraged, Holly sank down to the ground onto a bed of soft pine needles. Nothing in her life was the same as it used to be—her parents, Nick, Bonk. She'd never felt more miserable.

Leafy treetops swayed back and forth in the breeze above her. Holly zeroed in on them with her binoculars. In the wind, two branches opened like curtains on a stage. Behind them was a dying, leafless tree.

It was covered in whitewash!

She sat up. It looked as if someone had spilled white paint down the tree's side. She'd read about whitewash in that book. Whitewash was owl poop! Her eyes followed the white streaks. Some was splattered on the ground, too.

She didn't dare move.

Starting from the trunk, she studied every crooked and craggy branch going up, up, up. She saw woodpecker holes, dangling limbs, and then, there, in a large fork of the tree—a pile of sticks that looked like a monster head of uncombed hair. A stick nest!

An owl's nest? She squinted through the binoculars. Was anybody home? She stood up and backed away very slowly, trying not to make a sound. She climbed the hill and onto a big boulder to get a better view.

Standing there, she raised the binoculars to her eyes. She circled around until she zoomed in on the nest. Two soft brown eyes blinked open and peered out at her.

Holly gasped. "My owl."

She couldn't take her eyes from the nest. With all the sticks and twigs and the owl's speckled feathers, it was like trying to find a matching sock in a messy drawer.

Then she saw a ball of feathery fluff on a branch outside the nest. A baby owl? The pile of feathers shifted and became two. Two baby owls.

Two baby owls!?!? Holly's heart beat faster. She turned the eyepiece on the binoculars to focus. The owlets were all fuzz and fluff, their eyes wide open, full of questions, staring right at her. Mr. Owl did have a family. Or maybe Mr. Owl was a Mrs.?

A shadowy form circled above the trees. Holly held her breath as she followed the large owl's descent to the nest. Was that a mouse dangling from his mouth? With a mixture of amazement and horror, she watched as the owl ripped apart the mouse and fed it to the owlets.

Wow! Nick would never believe this! Holly gave a little jump. She had to find Nick right away. He had to see this!

As Holly took off she slipped on a patch of

wet moss and lost her footing. She tumbled to the ground, the binoculars knocking hard against the rock, shattering the plastic rim around an eyepiece.

Binoculars are an expensive instrument, not a toy.

Slowly, Holly raised the binoculars to her eyes. She pointed them toward the nest. She closed both eyes. She opened her right eye. The nest came into view. She opened her left eye. All she saw was darkness. She turned the binoculars around in her hands. The left eyeglass was gone.

Holly looked to the ground. There it sat, in a bed of leaves, a flash of glass, glinting like an angry eye. Her heart fell to her ankles.

Gram was going to kill her.

She picked the lens up from the leaves and put it in her pocket. She strapped the binoculars around her neck. She'd take them back and hide them in her room until she got a chance to talk to Mom. When Mom called tonight, she'd take the phone into her room so no one could listen. Mom would tell her what to do.

On the walk back to the house Holly noticed blood running down her shin. Oh, great. *You could get hurt,* Gram had warned.

Holly snuck back into the house. Gram was

doing a puzzle and listening to the radio and didn't notice a thing. In silent, slow motion, Holly crept up the stairs and into the bathroom. Carefully, she washed off her leg and bandaged her knee. She put on a pair of long sweatpants.

From now on she would stay away from the owls. She'd be very quiet and she'd be very good. Just like she'd promised Mom. She'd hang up her towels, stay close to home, and set the table even if it wasn't her turn. From now on, Holly would be perfect. No more sneaking out. And definitely no more looking for owls.

Chapter Fourteen

That night, when Mom called, Gram sent Holly and Nick outside to take Bonk on a slow and easy walk. She needed to have a private conversation, she said. "But why, Gram? Why can't we stay? Besides, I need to talk to her," Holly said. The scrape on her leg began to sting.

Gramp patted Holly's shoulder. "Not this time, okay, Hol'?"

Holly crossed her arms across her chest and didn't move. "This isn't right. A girl should have a chance to talk to her own mother."

"Nick?" Gramp said.

"Yeah, okay. I'll take her."

"You can talk to your mom later," said Gram.

As they walked down to the water, with Bonk limping along beside them, Holly turned to Nick. "Are Mom and Dad getting a divorce?" she asked.

"How should I know?"

"Cuz you're older. Maybe Gramp said something to you."

"Look, Holly, I don't know anything, okay?" He ran ahead of her. Holly stayed with Bonk, who took his time, limping down the path. By the time they made it to the dock, Nick had stripped down to his shorts and was swimming away with wild angry strokes.

He shouldn't be doing that, swimming on his own, when it was getting dark.

"Nick!" she called. "Nick, come back!"

But Nick kept swimming with lightening speed to the raft. He sat out there for a long time, in the middle of the raft, hugging his knees to his chest.

It seemed like forever that she sat waiting for him to come back. When he finally jumped up, dripping and out of breath, he said, "Don't tell Gram."

That was the last thing on her mind.

They waited on the dock until he dried off and got dressed. When they got back to the house, Gram and Gramp were done with the phone call. "Your mom and dad are going to stay on for the weekend at the Moose Lodge, then they're coming to pick you up."

"That's good news, right?" Holly asked.

Gram and Gramp exchanged a look. "Of course," Gram said. "Moose Lodge is a very nice place to stay."

• • •

"Thank you for helping without being asked," Gram said to Holly the next day.

"You're welcome," Holly said as she carried in the last bundle of groceries from the car. They'd come back from buying groceries in town. As Gram unloaded the bags, Holly helped. She placed boxes of cereal in a cabinet. She hung bananas on the banana hanger. She put the milk and juice in the fridge.

When she was done, she told Gram she was going to take her book outside to the hammock to read.

"Wait, Holly. Take these on your way out." Gram handed her the empty shopping bags.

"Where do you want me to put them?"

"In the mudroom. On one of the pegs by the binoculars. If you can find one." Gram laughed.

Binoculars? She drew in a deep breath and held it as she took the bags into the mudroom.

"Can you find a good place for them?" Gram called from the kitchen. "Or do I need to come clean out that disaster area and find a space for you?"

"Oh, no, Gram. There's plenty of space!" She hung the bags where the binoculars had been. Gram hadn't noticed they were missing.

The next gray afternoon, Holly looked on as Gramp and Nick played a game of chess. Outside, heavy gray clouds hung in the air.

"What's that piece called again?" Holly asked.

"Bishop," Gramp said.

"It moves diagonally, right?"

"But can't jump," said Gramp.

"And the piece that looks like a castle?"

"That's the rook."

"What does the rook do?"

"Holly, stop interrupting. Can't you see Gramp and I are in the middle of a game?" said Nick.

"Sorreeee," she said.

Gramp winked at her. "After our game's over, I'll show you some moves. Sound good?"

Gram looked up from her book. "Is somebody bored?" she asked. "We've got a couple of hours before supper, Holly. Let's go outside and see what birds we can add to your list." Gram made a move towards the mudroom.

Holly panicked. "That's okay, Gram. I have other stuff I can do."

"We've been stuck inside all afternoon. Come. Let's get the blood moving before the rain comes."

"No, really Gram. I feel like reading. Or working on my journal. Or, hey! Want to do a puzzle together?"

"Frank?" Gram called out from the mudroom. "Have you seen my binoculars? I always leave them right here on this hook."

"Can't say as I have," Gramp said. "When was the last time you had them?"

Holly heard Gram rummaging around in the mudroom. Then she came back to the living room. "The last time, I believe, was when Holly and I went out." Gram turned to Holly. "I put them back, didn't I?"

Holly shrugged. She took her book and escaped upstairs. As she climbed the steps, she heard Gram opening and closing cabinets and drawers.

"I'm sure they'll turn up somewhere," Gramp said. "You know how these things go at our age." He laughed.

Gram groaned.

"Check!" said Nick.

"Not again," said Gramp.

Upstairs, Holly climbed into bed, pulled up her quilt, and opened her book. She stared at the words on the page until they blurred. She couldn't read. She couldn't think. She couldn't do anything but wait for Mom and Dad to come get her, and hope Gram wouldn't find out about the binoculars. Mom? Dad? she whispered. Please hurry!

Chapter Fifteen

Finally, Holly's last night without Mom and Dad arrived. It was during suppertime when the winds began to howl. Outside, the skies went from light overcast gray to dark gloomy gray before Holly had finished her plate of chicken and rice. "Big storm coming," Gramp said. "They're predicting rain all night and through tomorrow."

Gram got up and started closing windows.

Thunder rumbled in the distance. "Nick, run outside and check that I closed the car windows," Gramp said.

The wind sucked the door shut behind Nick and slammed it with a bang. The lights flickered on and off.

"Holly, in that drawer over there. Bring out the candles," Gramp said.

"It's really coming down," Nick said when he

came back in the house, rain dripping off his face.

"Oh boy!" Gramp said, slapping his thighs. "Nothing I like better than a good storm."

Gram groaned. "Until the power goes out," she said.

Holly lined the candles up on the table. She picked at the rest of the food on her plate. Maybe Gramp loved a storm, but seeing the trees whip back and forth outside made her nervous. What about the owlets? Would they be able to hang on in their nest?

Just then, the phone rang. Gram answered. "Hi, Valerie. Has this awful storm come your way, too?"

Holly stood next to Gram, waiting her turn to talk.

"Hm-m-m. That bad?" Gram asked. She turned to Gramp and whispered, "River's up. The lodge road's washed out."

Holly felt more and more jumpy inside. "Can I talk to Mom now?" she asked. "Please?"

Gram looked at Holly and lifted a finger to her lips. "Oh, sure, the kids are fine. We're all cozied in for the storm. You know your father. Not to worry," she said into the phone.

Outside, lightning crashed through the stormy skies. Bonk whimpered and hid under the table. "Valerie, there's lightning here. I'm going to hang up now." Gram returned the phone to its cradle.

"But Gram, I wanted to talk!" Holly cried. She thought of the binoculars buried in her bottom drawer, the owlets in their nest. She had to see Mom. Had to see Mom and Dad.

"Not with this lightning," said Gram.

"Can't I call her back? Please? It's really important."

Another crack of lightning shot through the air.

"Too dangerous to use a phone during lightning," Gram said.

"Can I use your cell phone?"

"No coverage here."

The electricity shut down. The house went dark.

"Light the candles, Nick," Gramp said.

"Mom and Dad are still coming tomorrow, aren't they?" Holly asked.

"'Fraid not," Gram said. "The road's impassable. Until it gets fixed, they're stuck at the lodge."

"But I've been waiting all this time. I need to see my mom." Her voice came out all wobbly.

"You'll be fine, Holly. We'll all be fine. It's just a summer storm," said Gramp.

Holly curled up next to Bonk while Gramp made a fire in the fireplace. "It's okay, Bonky. Everything's going to be okay," she said over and over again, stroking his fur. But the more she said it, the more unsure she became.

All that dark night, the rain came down in torrents. It splattered and pinged and bounced off the screens in Holly's windows. It coursed down her skylight like a raging river. It drummed against the metal roof like thousands of galloping horses. Between the booming thunder and crackling lightning, the rain was everywhere and all the time.

Holly snuggled tightly under her calico quilt. "Great night for sleeping," Gramp had said. Not for Holly. She kept imagining Mom and Dad on the other side of a washed-out road, unable to cross to come back to her at Padgett Lake. She kept imagining Gram hunting for the binoculars and finding them in her messy bureau drawer. She kept imagining the owlets in a rain-soaked nest, huddled together, shivering, wet, and alone.

Chapter Sixteen

The next morning, a slice of sunlight slanted through Holly's window and fell across her eyes. Holly awoke with a start. Her first thought was: Mom and Dad. Then, that awful word—separation. Then she thought: the baby owls! Was the owl family safe?

No one was up yet. The house was quiet. Holly got out of bed and put on her flip-flops. She looked out the window. A mess of broken branches and twigs and leaves were scattered all around the ground. She grabbed her calico quilt and wrapped it around her shoulders.

She crept silently down the stairs, making sure to avoid the creaky stair that might wake Gram up. She'd rush down the road, check on the owlets, and be back before anyone knew she was gone.

Holly snuck out and set off down the road.

Trees were down and broken branches criss-crossed the lawn, but the early morning sun turned the raindrops still hanging on the leaves into dazzling jewels. The sky was the brightest blue Holly had ever seen, as if the storm had washed it clean. Slowly, bird voices began to fill the air.

She turned into the woods to find the owls' nest. She tied her quilt around her shoulders so she could have both arms free to push back broken tree limbs that dangled from trees. She climbed onto her sighting rock and squinted her eyes to where the nest should be.

Half of it was gone.

Holly slid off the rock. She crept toward the base of the owl tree. Sticks from the nest were strewn everywhere, all over the ground.

The babies! Where were the babies? She moved closer, studying every wet clump of leaves and dip in the land. "Where are you, little owlets?" Holly whispered. "Where are you?"

She couldn't keep the sinking feeling out of her stomach: maybe the baby owls couldn't fly. Maybe the parents were out hunting for food and didn't get back. Maybe some animal had eaten them up.

Holly kept looking and looking. She looked behind rocks covered with lichen but only found sticks and leaves. She looked under a piece of rotting bark but only found worms and beetles.

Then, over by the pile of sticks, something moved on the ground.

The owlets. Holly gasped. Their puffy feathers were now matted, dirty, and wet. Holly moved nearer. Was that trembling she saw? Yes! They were still alive.

Oh, but they must be so cold and scared. Poor babies. Poor, poor little owlet babies. Where were the parents? They shouldn't have left their babies in a storm!

"Don't worry, little owlets. I'll take care of you."

She untied the quilt from around her shoulders and stepped closer. Cupping her hands together under a corner of the quilt, she gently scooped up the first owlet and placed it at the other end of the quilt. She picked up the second owlet and laid it right next to him. She fluffed the quilt around them. "All cozy now?" she asked. One's small beak opened and he let out short whiney peeps. The other's chin jiggled but no sound came.

Of course! The owlets must be hungry! Holly kicked the rotting bark off the log. She broke a piece that was crawling with bugs and beetles and laid it on the blanket next to the owlets. Then she watched and waited. Waited for the babies to eat.

The owlets didn't move. She used a twig to push the bugs in their direction. But still the owlets didn't eat.

Then, high above the treetops, Holly sensed some movement. Two owls circled overhead. The mother and father! They'd come back!

She looked down at the scraggly owlets on her quilt. She looked above to the big owls looping in the sky. And, suddenly, standing there on this quiet morning, between the owlets and the owls, she began to feel quite small. Just like that day at the lake—she was just one small girl in a huge world.

But she was part of it, too.

Her quilt could suffocate the owlets. And she didn't really know what owlets ate. Maybe worms and beetles weren't enough. Owls ate mice and rodents, didn't they? "Owls are not like those cartoon characters you kids watch on television," Gram had said. "They're wild animals."

The owls circled lower.

She remembered the poster in Dr. Davis's office. Found an injured or orphaned animal? Leave it alone! Call a Licensed Wildlife Rehabilitator.

Holly dashed out of the woods and onto the road. If she wanted to save these owls, she couldn't do it alone.

Chapter Seventeen

"I have to call Dr. Davis," Holly said, rushing through the door. Coffee smells filled the air and the radio played soft music.

"Holly, where on earth have you been?" Gram asked. "I thought you were still in bed."

"Do you have the number?" Holly asked, going to the phone.

"I said, young lady, where have you been?" Gram said.

"Gram, the owls are in trouble. I…." She went through the list of numbers by the phone.

"Owls? You were out looking for owls again? At this hour? In your pajamas?" Gram said.

"Gram, please. This is important." There it was. Dr. Davis. 555-0297.

Gram drew in a deep breath and let it out slowly. Like she was getting ready for a big talking-to. She placed her hand over the phone. "I expressly told you not to leave the house without telling someone. I told you…."

"I found owlets. They fell out of their nest. In the storm," Holly said.

"Owlets? When did you find owlets? I didn't know about…."

Again, Holly interrupted. "The baby owls are on the ground, but they're alive. We have to try to save them."

Gram cocked her head and looked at Holly. Her eyebrows knit together. Her lips pursed. But she handed Holly the phone.

Holly pressed the "talk" button and waited for the dial tone. She pressed it again and again. "What's wrong with this phone?" she yelled. "It doesn't work!"

Gram took the phone from her and listened. "The phone lines must be down."

"But what about the owls? We have to do something."

"Show me where they are, Holly. Let's go."

"Oh, thank you, Gram. Thank you." Holly took Gram's hand and pulled her to the door.

"Wait. I'll need gloves in case we have to pick

them up. And let me dig through this mess one more time for my binoculars."

Just then, Nick came down the stairs, yawning, in his pajamas. "What's going on?"

"Nothing," Holly said.

"Where are you going?" Nick asked.

Gram found her gloves and put them in a pocket. She searched through the bags and jackets hanging on the pegs for the binoculars.

"Nowhere!" Holly shouted at Nick this time. She tugged at Gram's hand. Bonk stuck his nose between them, ready to follow.

"Bonk, stay!" Holly yelled at him.

Reluctantly, Bonk tucked his back legs underneath him to sit.

"And we don't have time to look for those binoculars, Gram. We have to go. Now!" She pulled Gram out the door.

"My goodness," said Gram.

Holly let go of Gram's hand and went off down the road ahead of her.

When they got to the sighting rock, she pointed out the sticks from the nest and the red flash of her quilt on the ground. She told Gram how she'd put the owlets on the quilt and how she'd hoped to feed them until she saw the owls circling overhead.

Gram said, "So the parents are still around. That's a good sign. We really need to wait for a wildlife rehabilitation specialist, but let me have a look at what's going on here first."

"You sure know a lot about owls, Gram."

"There's always something to learn at Padgett Lake. That's why I love it here."

"Me, too," said Holly.

"I know you do," said Gram.

They moved closer to the quilt. "See? There're the babies," Holly said.

"One's not moving," Gram said.

"He's probably resting."

"No, Holly, I'm afraid he's probably dead."

"That can't be," Holly cried. "I was just here. They were both alive."

"Nature sometimes holds life in a delicate balance."

"We should've come sooner. I should've made him eat something. I shouldn't have put the quilt down, I shouldn't have bothered them." Holly's eyes filled with tears.

Gram curled an arm around her. "No, Holly. Sometimes these things happen. Maybe that owl was born weaker, smaller. Maybe it fell harder to the ground. Maybe even if there hadn't been a storm, that owlet wouldn't have survived. What you did, or didn't do, couldn't have saved him."

Together, they went to the quilt. Gram put on her gloves and lifted the dead owlet onto a piece of bark.

"Can we bury him?" Holly whispered.

"Of course we can. But first let's get this little fellow back in what's left of the nest."

Holly eyed the tree. "I could climb up those branches and you could hand him to me."

"Great idea. You take the gloves. I'll lift him in the quilt."

Holly used the lower branches as steps to climb up the tree. She bent over to receive the owlet from Gram. She reached up and gently laid the owl in the nest. "Good luck, little owlet," she whispered, and then came down.

"Let's move away," Gram said.

They went back to the sighting rock. Gram used her hands to clear away leaves and a large stick to dig into the soil. Holly helped until they had a hole big enough for the dead owlet. She lowered the owlet on the piece of bark into the earth and covered it with dirt. Gram piled some stones on the grave. "Rest in peace, little owlet," she said, patting the stones in place.

"Rest in peace," Holly repeated. She added more stones and a handful of small pinecones.

As they sat together on the rock waiting for the owls, Holly said, "Gram, what's going to happen to Bonk? Is he really going to die like Nick said?"

"I suspect Bonk still has some good years left to him, but yes, Holly, some day he will die. All living things must die sometime."

"I'll be sad when Bonk dies."

"Me, too," said Gram.

Gram was being so nice, helping with the owlet, talking about Bonk. Maybe now Gram would understand about the binoculars. "Gram?"

"Are you sad about your owlet? I am."

"No. I mean yes. But that's not what I was going to say. She took a deep breath. "You know how you couldn't find your binoculars?"

"Yes?"

"Well, it was me. I took them. I know I shouldn't have. But I wanted...you know...the owls...and, Gram? I'm sorry. I'm really, really sorry."

"So you snuck out *and* you took my binoculars?"

"I wasn't thinking. I saw them on the peg and I took them. I know I shouldn't have."

"Where are they?"

If only she could shrink and disappear. Anything instead of answering that question. No matter how she arranged the words in her head, nothing seemed right.

"Holly?"

Might as well blurt it out and get it over with. "I broke them. I'll pay to get them fixed. Really I will. I promise. And if they can't get fixed, I'll buy you a new pair."

"That pair was very expensive." Gram stared down hard at Holly.

"I'll use my birthday money. I'll do jobs around the house. Don't worry, Gram, I'll take care of it."

"Indeed you will," Gram said, nodding her head ever so slightly, eyeing Holly with a dark stare.

"Are Mom and Dad going to get a divorce?"

"Why, Holly! You're certainly full of surprises today."

"I heard you talking to Gramp. On the porch."

Gram's face tightened.

"Well, are they? Getting a divorce?" Holly asked.

Gram sighed. "Sometimes marriages take a wrong turn, Holly. And it's hard to find a way back."

"Will my mom and dad find a way back?"

Gram patted Holly on the knee. "They're working on it. That much I know. I'm worried about them, too, just like you are. But I think they truly love each other and they love you and Nick. So, yes, I believe in them. I'm pretty sure they can work something out."

Gram had never talked to her like this before, like she wasn't a little kid that you had to hide things from.

"You do know, Holly, that when parents have troubles, it's between them. It's not the children's fault. You do know that, right?"

"Everyone knows that." She picked lichen off the rock and crunched it in her palm. Of course everyone knew that.

Gram pulled Holly close. Holly rested her head against Gram's shoulder. For a moment, they sat in silence.

"Oh, look!" Gram pointed into the sky. "The owls are back. The owlet doesn't need us now that the parents have returned. I think we'd better move away, don't you?"

"Oh yes." Holly nodded. "Owls are very protective of their young."

Holly and Gram stood at a distance and watched in silence as an adult owl swooped into the nest, a mouse dangling from its mouth, and fed it to the owlet.

Chapter Eighteen

Later that afternoon, while Holly and Nick were playing Monopoly, Bonk started barking.

"They're here!" Holly cried. "Mom and Dad are here!"

"They're not going to come for another hour." Nick rolled the dice for his turn at Monopoly.

"Yes, they are. Bonk hears them." Holly ran to the door and went outside with Bonk. Down the road the sound of car tires on gravel grew louder. Soon, Mom and Dad's car turned in the drive. "Mom! Dad!" she cried.

Nick came outside, followed by Gram and Gramp. When the car stopped and Mom and Dad got out, Holly ran up to hug them. "Did you have a good time?" asked Mom. "How's my girl?" said Dad. His beard was scratchy against Holly's cheek when he kissed her. Mom was wearing a new dress

Holly had never seen before.

"Did you grow another foot?" Dad asked Nick.

"Hey, kiddo," Mom said, giving him a hug.

Soon everyone was talking. About the pine chest, the fishing trip, the blueberry pies. Bonk's trip to the vet, all the dragonflies this year, the perfect temperature of the lake.

"I could use a swim," said Dad. "Do we have time before dinner?"

"Plenty of time," said Gram. "Holly, show your Mom and Dad how you can swim to the raft."

"Swim to the raft?" Mom asked.

"You're swimming to the raft now? By yourself?" Dad said.

"Your daughter has grown up quite a bit in these two weeks," Gram said, winking at Holly. "Haven't you, Holly?"

Holly nodded. She could swim to the raft, she'd played her first game of chess, she'd helped save the owls. But she'd felt most grown up when she and Gram started talking, telling the truth even though it was hard. Asking questions and listening to the answers even though they weren't what she wanted to hear. Grownup talking.

"It's not like you to be so quiet," Dad said. "Cat

got your tongue?"

Holly shrugged. She felt strangely shy around her parents.

"Are you okay?" Mom asked.

Mom's question jerked Holly out of her shyness. "Me okay? What about you?" She looked up at her mom. "Are you okay, Mom?" she asked. Then she looked over to her dad. "Are you okay?"

Mom and Dad glanced at each other. Dad took Mom's hand. Mom smiled at him. "Yeah, we're okay. Still working on it," Mom said.

"Three-quarters of the way there," Dad said.

"Almost home," said Mom.

• • •

Holly and Bonk were the first ones back in the house after the swim. Gramp and Nick were showing Mom and Dad the big pile of wood they'd split together. Holly didn't need to hear—again—about how big and strong Nick was becoming. She strode into the kitchen and stopped short when she saw the dining table.

The placemats didn't match. The napkins were folded into little tepees on the plates. The utensils zigzagged their way in a circular design around the table. The water glasses were all upside down.

"Gram!" Holly said. "What did you do?"

"It's Sunday supper. On Sunday you can set the table any way you want," Gram said, humming as she set a frying pan full of bread in the middle of the table.

Holly put a spoon and a stick of butter in a cereal bowl. "What about the butter, Gram? Where do you think it wants to go?"

Together they stared at the dining table. With six plates and glasses and utensils all over the place, there wasn't room for one more thing.

"We'd better think before we act," Holly said.

"Oh, I think this time we'd better let our imaginations carry us away," Gram said.

Bonk wagged his tail, and outside, far down the road, as the moon, almost full now, rose in the sky, an owl seemed to agree. *Hoo-hoo, hoo-hoo; hoo-hoo, hoo-hoo-aww*, he called.

Hoo-hoo, hoo-hoo; hoo-hoo, hoo-hoo-aww.

Acknowledgments

Thank you to all the faculty, staff, and students at Vermont College for Fine Arts, and especially to my advisors Kathi Appelt, David Gifaldi, Marion Dane Bauer, Deborah Wiles, and Rita Williams-Garcia. Thanks also to my classmates, The Dedications.

Thank you to fellow writers Toni Buzzeo, Jacqueline Davies, Tracey Fern, Jennifer Jacobson, Sarah Lamstein, Cynthia Lord, Carol Peacock, and Dana Walrath. You've cheered me on through the years in critique groups and on retreat. I am truly grateful for your expertise, enthusiasm, and support.

Thank you to Jamie Hogan for capturing the spirit of Owl Girl is her amazing cover illustration, and to the fine people at Maine Authors Publishing for turning Owl Girl into a book.

Big hugs and kisses and much love to my family: Adam, Amanda, and Steve. You're the best!